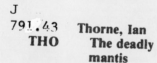

THE DEADLY MANTIS

BY IAN THORNE
ADAPTED FROM A SCREENPLAY BY MARTIN BERKELEY

EDITED BY
DR. HOWARD SCHROEDER
Professor in Reading and Language Arts
Dept. of Elementary Education
Mankato State University

Copyright© 1982 by MCA Publishing, a Division of MCA INC. All rights reserved.

Library of Congress Catalog Card Number: 81-22074

International Standard Book Numbers:
0-89686-214-3 Library Bound
0-89686-217-8 Paperback

Design - Tammy Loe

Library of Congress Cataloging in Publication Data
Thorne, Ian. Adapted from a screenplay by Martin Berkeley.
  The deadly mantis.

  (Monster series)
  SUMMARY: A giant insect frozen for millions of years thaws out in Alaska and
makes its way to New York City.
  (1. Monsters--Fiction. 2. Horror--Fiction) I. Berkeley, Martin. II. Schroeder,
Howard. III. Title. IV. Series: Thorne, Ian. Monster Series.
PZ7.T3927De   (Fic)   81-22074
ISBN 0-89686-214-3 (lib. bdg.)   AACR2
ISBN 0-89686-217-8 (pbk.)

PHOTOGRAPHIC CREDITS

Universal City Studios: 6, 8-9, 11, 12-13, 14-15, 17, 18-19, 20, 21, 22, 23, 28, 29, 36, 38,
42, 43, 44, 45, 46-47
Forrest J. Ackerman: 16, 24, 26, 30, 31, 32, 34-35, 37, 40-41

Published by arrangement with MCA PUBLISHING,
A Division of MCA INC.

MCA PUBLISHING, a Division of MCA INC.
100 Universal City Plaza
Universal City, California 91608
Published by
CRESTWOOD HOUSE, INC.
Highway 66 South
P.O. Box 3427
Mankato, Minnesota 56002-3427
Printed in the United States of America

THE DEADLY MANTIS

BY IAN THORNE
ADAPTED FROM A SCREENPLAY BY MARTIN BERKELEY

TROUBLE IN THE ARTIC

Lt. Col. Joe Parkman was very worried.

"Try to contact the weather base again," he told his radio operator.

"Red Eagle One calling Weather Four! Come in, Weather Four." The radio man waited a long time for an answer. "No reply sir," he told Joe.

Joe frowned. A patrol plane had flown over the weather base not long before. Its pilot reported that the roof of the building seemed to be smashed in. No people could be seen. And now the weather base did not respond to the call.

What could have happened? There had been no storms in that area. Weather Four was an outpost of the DEW Line — the Distant Early Warning network of radar stations. It was located on the frozen Arctic Ocean, miles from any settlement. Its radar searched the sky for weather data and also kept watch against invading Russian aircraft that might try to fly over the North Pole.

Did the Russians have something to do with the trouble at Weather Four? Joe Parkman felt his blood run cold. The year was 1956, and the DEW Line was brand new. Joe was the commander of an Air Force Interceptor Base that was part of the Line. If Russians invaded North America, Joe's men would be the first to meet the enemy. He would have to see what had gone wrong at Weather Four himself. America's security might depend on it.

"Get my plane ready!" Joe ordered.

At his desk, Lt. Col. Joe Parkman (Craig Stevens) receives news of trouble.

Joe Parkman and his aide (Paul Campbell) investigate the weather station.

Joe Parkman and Lt. Fred Pizarro flew a skiplane to Weather Four. They discovered that one wall was pushed in, and the roof was partly torn off. There was no sign of the men who should have been on duty.

Fred shook his head in disbelief. "Two men don't just vanish!"

Joe examined the wreckage as he spoke. "But they did. Not a trace of them! And no sign of whatever did this damage."

"Looks like a plane hit the roof," said Fred. "But

where is it?"

The wind howled through the broken roof and walls. Snow covered the equipment.

"No blood, no footprints, nothing," said Fred. "I guess we can't blame the Russians for this, Colonel."

"No," Joe agreed. "It doesn't look like it. Perhaps it was a freak storm that didn't show on our radar. A small tornado, maybe. That might have caused this kind of damage."

"But that can't explain the missing men," Fred said.

Joe and Frank examined the snowy ice around the wrecked hut.

"Here's something funny," Joe said bending down. He had discovered two ruts in the snow. They were like the skid marks made by an aircraft. "But no plane ever made that short a takeoff run."

"A chopper?" Fred suggested.

"Look at the edges of the ruts. They have strange little prints — almost like feathers! No helicopter did this."

"Then what did?" Fred asked. But Joe had no answer. There was nothing the two men could do but return to the base.

A day later there was more trouble. A cargo plane from Alaska had disappeared off the radar. Joe sent out search planes. They spotted wreckage.

Once again Joe Parkman and Fred Pizarro went to examine the scene. The wreck was on snow-covered ice.

"This plane was smashed from above!" Joe exclaimed. "See? This damage could not have been caused by the crash. This is another strange one, Fred." He poked through the torn metal. There were no bodies.

"Look at this!" Joe cried suddenly.

What can it be?

He had found a weird object. It was flat and greenish colored, and as tall as a man. One end was pointed.

"What in the world is it?" Fred asked.

Joe lifted the thing up. It did not weigh much. "I've never seen anything like it before," Joe said. "It's almost like a tooth or a claw. But it can't be. See how one end is broken?"

"Some kind of gunk is coming out the broken end," Fred noted. "What'll we do with it?"

"Take it back to the base," Joe decided. "I want Dr. Carver to have a look at it."

The base doctor (David McMahon) is mystified by Joe's find.

Joe called the base doctor to examine the mystery object as soon as he returned.

"What do you think, Doc?" Joe inquired.

The doctor shook his head. He touched the gooey matter that dripped from the thing's broken end.

"This isn't bone," Dr. Carver said. "And it's much too large to be a tooth or a claw. I just don't know."

"Could this thing have had anything to do with the crash of the cargo plane?" Joe asked.

"You've got me," the doctor replied.

Joe looked grim. "We'll send it to NORAD. General Ford will have to decide what to do next."

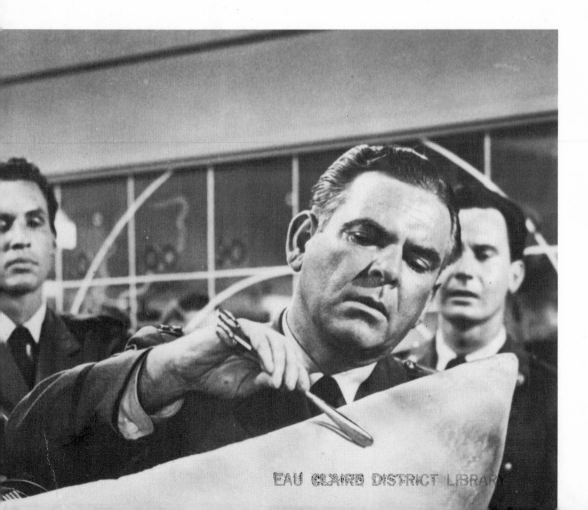

Dr. Ned Jackson (William Hopper) and Marge Blaine (Alix Talton) do not know that adventure awaits them in the Arctic.

THE MYSTERY DEEPENS

Some days later, in a city thousands of miles south of the Arctic, a scientist sat in his office in a large museum. On his desk was a small skeleton which he carefully studied.

There was a knock on the door.

"Come in," called Dr. Ned Jackson still tinkering with the skeleton. "Oh, hello, Marge."

Marge Blaine, who was in charge of the museum's magazine, came into the office to show Ned some photos. "What have you got there?" she asked. "Another fossil?"

"No," he replied. "One of the kids in my junior

science group mounted this cat skelton. But he forgot some of the bones."

"How can you tell?" Marge asked. "It looks fine to me. Four legs, tail, ribs and stuff."

Ned laughed. "It's the business of a paleontologist to know! Now look very closely."

He stopped as the phone rang. "Hello? Yes, this is Jackson. What? The Pentagon is calling?"

Marge stood open-mouthed while Ned listened to the voice on the phone. Then he said, "I'll come right away," and hung up. "I have to go to Washington, Marge. Something about a mystery bone from the North Pole!"

Ned examines the mystery object while General Ford (Donald Randolph) and Dr. Gunther (Florenz Ames) await his solution.

When Ned Jackson arrived at the Pentagon, he found General Ford and another scientist, Dr. Gunther, examining the "bone."

It did not take Ned long to discover that the strange object had once been part of a living thing. But what kind of a creature?

"This material is not true bone," Ned said. "It seems more like part of an insect."

"Dr. Gunther has tried to analyze the matter inside that thing," General Ford said. "But he can't tell what it might be."

"Let's take it to the museum," Ned suggested. "We can do more extensive tests there."

General Ford agreed to Ned's suggestion. After a day or two, Ned and Gunther had the answer.

The strange object was indeed part of an insect. But that insect had to be the biggest one the world had ever seen! Marge Blaine heard about the discovery and came to see Ned.

"What's this about a giant bug?" she asked.

"It's true," Dr. Gunther told her. "The thing found in the Arctic was the spur (wings or legs) of a huge insect. Ages ago, there were enormous insects on Earth. Now it seems that at least one giant fossil insect has come to life!"

"A mantis," Ned said. "One of the fiercest, most deadly insects of all."

Ned shows Dr. Gunther a fossil insect preserved in amber. He suspects that the mystery insect was preserved in ice.

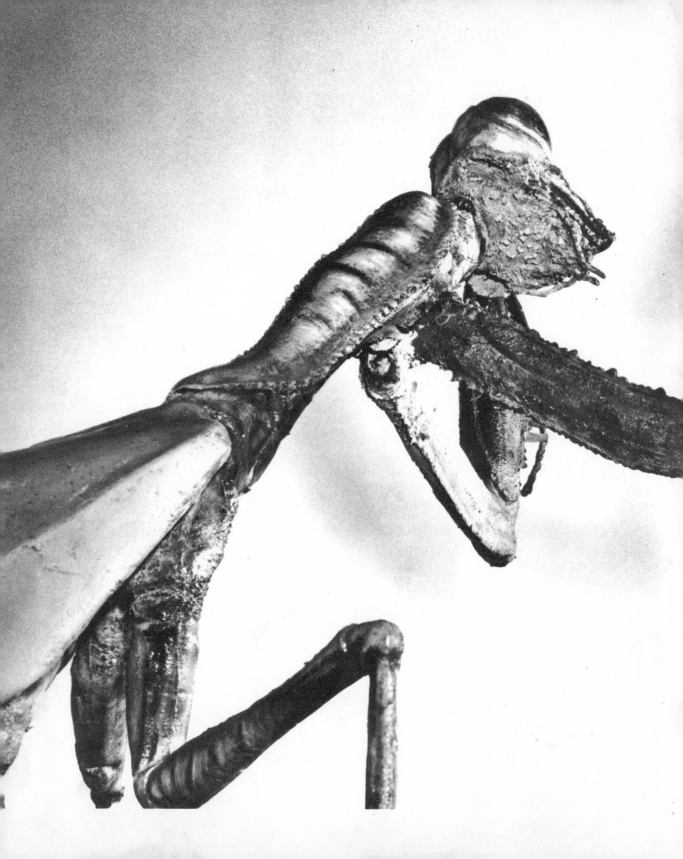

Ned opened a book for Marge. "Here's a picture of one. Today's mantises are small. Only two to five inches long. But they're fierce little critters. They hold their legs up like they're praying and then pounce. The front legs have sharp spines to hold the victim. Mantises eat their food alive."

"But this spine you have is huge!" Marge exclaimed in horror. "And the insect it came from . . ."

Ned finished for her. "Must be bigger than a house. That's why the Air Force has asked me to come to the Arctic to investigate. I'm leaving today."

"You'll need a photographer," said Marge. "I'm ready to go when you are."

MENACE FROM THE PAST

Ned and Marge flew north to the Arctic Interceptor Base. Col. Joe Parkman welcomed them.

"I hope you can help us solve our mystery," Joe said.

"We'll do our best," Ned assured him.

"There's been another report of a strange attack," Joe said. "An Eskimo village was terrorized and one man was killed. The people say it was an evil spirit. A giant monster. That's nonsense, of course."

"Don't be too sure," said Ned.

Joe welcomes Ned and Marge to the Arctic Base.

Joe and Ned measure the marks left by the mysterious creature.

Joe Parkman flew Ned and Marge to the scene of the crashed cargo plane. They looked at odd skid marks in the snow.

"We found marks like this next to the weather station that was destroyed," Joe said. "There were more of them at the Eskimo village."

"Eight and a half feet!" exclaimed Marge, as Ned measured the skidlike track.

"What does it mean, Dr. Jackson?" asked Joe.

"Let's get back to the base," said Ned, "and I'll try to explain."

The bleak arctic night closed in. The Air Force base, located in the midst of a snowy wilderness, was snug and warm. Cheerful lights shone from its windows. Music could be heard coming from the recreation hall. In one room of the base, Ned Jackson did his calculations. He explained to Joe Parkman that he believed a giant insect was at large — killing people because there was nothing else for it to eat in the wasteland.

Outside in the snowy night, inhuman eyes were studying the lighted buildings. The enormous creature was very hungry.

Inside the base, Ned was saying, "I know a giant insect seems impossible, Col. Parkman. But millions of years ago, there were dragonflies three feet wide."

"That was millions of years ago," Joe said dryly.

"The evidence points to a giant mantis," Ned said firmly. "Perhaps it was frozen into a block of ice ages ago. And now, for some reason, it's been released. Perhaps there was a volcanic eruption deep under the Arctic Ocean."

"Why haven't we seen the thing?" Joe asked.

"Mantises can fly," Ned replied. "There are lots of hiding places among the arctic ice floes. Or . . ."

Suddenly, Marge Blaine screamed. "At the window!"

It's outside the window!

There was a sound of breaking glass. Marge yelled again. A huge insect claw, bristling with deadly spines, thrust into the room. The people fled.

"Sound the alarm!" Joe Parkman cried.

There was a great crash. The building rocked. The lights blinked. Overhead, the roof began to creak and bend downward. Joe reached an intercom.

"Condition Red!" he yelled into the mike. "Get all planes airborne at once! This is Col. Parkman speaking! Condition Red!"

Marge and Ned ran to safety as the roof in that part of the air base began to collapse. Men grabbed their weapons, threw on parkas, and raced outside.

They could not believe what they saw.

The searchlight for the airfield was turned on. There in the strong beam of light was a towering form. It had a pointed head with rounded, gleaming eyes. Its arms were like the blades of knives, all studded with cruel spines. The creature hopped from the roof of a crushed hut and attacked a group of men.

The airmen fired round after round of bullets from their rifles. The mantis kept coming. One man raised a machine gun and began to fire. The mantis uttered an angry hiss. Then it roared! Its wings began to beat, making a terrible humming sound.

"It's taking off!" somebody yelled. "Look out!"

The men fell flat. There was a great blast of wind . . . and when the men looked up, the giant mantis had disappeared.

Terrified airmen fire at the deadly mantis.

THE MANTIS FLIES SOUTH

The planes from the Interceptor Base searched in vain for the deadly mantis. There was no sign of it.

But a Canadian radar station, hundreds of miles to the south, reported an odd blip. It was not an aircraft. It was very low in the air, out over the stormy sea.

"Could it be the mantis?" Marge asked Ned Jackson.

The mantis seeks fresh victims at sea.

"Perhaps the creature's instinct is leading it south," the scientist said. "Mantises are mostly found in the tropics. Perhaps this huge thing is trying to return to its ancient home, the jungle it left millions of years ago."

Ned's guess was right. But before the mantis could reach a warm climate, it would stop for food along the way.

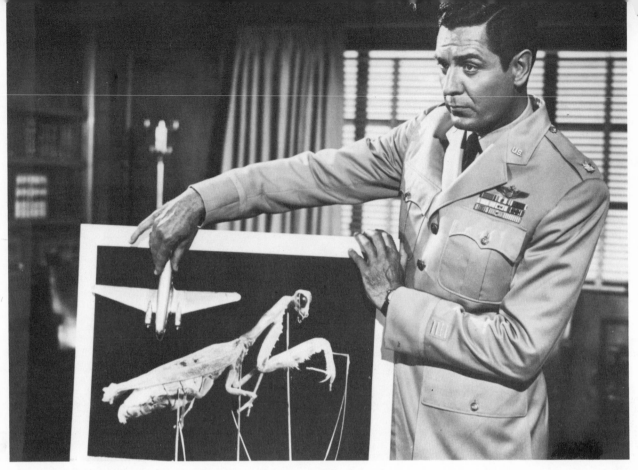

Speaking on TV, Joe shows the size of the mantis.

Marge and Ned could do no more in the Arctic. They flew home to Washington, D.C. Col. Joe Parkman went south with them. He was needed to help organize a defense against the deadly insect.

Joe appeared on television to explain the danger. "I saw this creature attack our base," Joe said. "It's real, not a dream."

He showed a picture of an ordinary mantis. "This is what the thing looks like. Normally, a mantis is only a few inches long. But this mantis is not normal."

Joe held up the model of a C-47 airplane. The mantis was almost twice as long.

"We believe that this giant insect is now flying south over the Atlantic Ocean," Joe said. "Some ships are reported missing. The mantis may have attacked them. And it may decide to come ashore at any time. Keep alert. Watch the sky and don't panic. If you see this thing, notify your local police or Air Force Base. Thank you."

Later, Joe got together with Ned and Marge. They tried to plot the course of the mantis on a map. "It could be in our area already," Ned said.

"I'm so tired," Marge said, "that I don't care. Will you drive me home?"

"Of course," said Joe.

Marge tries to plot the mantis's path on a map.

As Joe and Marge drove along a foggy road, they listened to the radio. News of a nearby train wreck was broadcast.

"That's close by!" Marge exclaimed. "Do you think it could be the work of the mantis?"

Joe laughed. "I hardly think so. But we'll have a look."

They reached the wreck. The police thought it was just an ordinary accident. Marge sighed. "I suppose they're right," she said.

She and Joe got back into the car. They never noticed the strange skidmarks in the dust beside the railroad tracks . . .

A strange wreck attracts spectators.

Marge and Joe see a distraught woman led from the wreck.

They drove on. The fog became thicker. Suddenly, the radio said: "We interrupt to present this news flash! A bus has just been demolished in a mystery accident along Arlington Road!"

Joe made a quick U-turn and raced off to the scene of the accident. He and Marge found a bus flipped over on its side. A woman passenger was screaming.

Joe got out to see what had happened.

"The driver's body is missing," he said.

"I was his last passenger!" the woman wept. "He told me to be careful! And the thing . . . the terrible thing . . ." She fell into the arms of a state trooper.

"Let's get out of here," Joe said to Marge.

31

THE MANTIS IN NEW YORK

After its attack on the bus, the mantis struck again. It menaced the area around Washington, D.C. The Air Force sent fighter jets to attack the deadly insect. The plane fired rockets at it and drove it out to sea.

But they could not shoot it down.

The mantis could fly faster than a jet plane. It winged off northeast, and it dropped so low that it could not be picked up by radar.

Ned was with General Ford at the mantis defense headquarters in the Pentagon.

"We've lost it!" exclaimed the general.

"What can you do about it?" Ned asked.

"We can hope that a member of the Ground Observer Team will spot the thing," said Ford. "It's certain to head back to land."

Col. Joe Parkman was in the air with the squadron pursuing the mantis. His radio crackled with a new report. "Mantis sighted over Baltimore!"

Moments later, there was another report: "Mantis over Newark!"

The jets screamed through the sky. Joe sighted the mantis and yelled, "There it is!" He peeled off to attack.

Rockets slammed into the flying mantis. The thing faltered in the air. Then it headed straight for Joe's plane! The plane and the giant insect collided in midair. Joe barely had time to pop the canopy and parachute to safety.

Joe is determined to finish the mantis.

The mantis fluttered down. Below was the city of New York. Joe's plane fell into the East River. He landed safely near the docks and was rescued by the police.

"Is it dead?" was the first question he asked.

"No," a policeman told him. "It's wounded. It went into the Manhattan Tunnel under the river. We're trying to smoke it out."

Hours went by. After a brief rest, Joe went to the tunnel. He found General Ford there, together with Ned and Marge.

Smashed autos littered the tunnel entrance.

"We've got the tunnel sealed off at the other end," the general said. "Volunteers are getting ready to go in after it."

"I'm going, too!" said Joe. "I've got a right to be in at the finish of that thing if any man has!"

The general explained that they were hoping to try to kill the mantis with poison gas. "If he smashes the tunnel," the general said, "we'll have a flood on our hands. We'll have to get him now."

From inside the tunnel came the roar of the deadly mantis.

General Ford tells Joe to be careful in the tunnel.

"I'm ready," Joe told the general.

"Good luck, Joe!" said Marge. She had tears in her eyes as Joe waved to her and went to brief his men.

The volunteers were all Air Force men, dressed in gas-proof suits. "You've been told what we have to do," Joe said. "The smoke will give us cover, and so will the cars that the mantis overturned inside the tunnel. The gas bombs will only work in a limited area. Wait for my signal before you throw them. Everybody ready?"

"Ready!" said all the men.

"Then let's go after it," said Joe. He led the way into the tunnel.

Where is it?

Cautiously, they made their way into the smoke. Inside the tunnel the huge creature was uttering its unearthly screeches. It was badly wounded. Joe knew that any mistake was likely to be fatal.

They trudged along. Smashed cars and trucks were everywhere . . . but there were no bodies. The mantis had been hungry, and it had found food.

"Let's hope we're not dessert!" Joe muttered to himself.

The tunnel lights shone dimly in the thick smoke. Then suddenly the men came into an area where the smoke was less dense. Many of the tunnel lights in this section had gone out. Ahead lay blackness.

The screeches of the mantis echoed from the tunnel walls. The men were sweating inside their heavy suits. Was it the heat — or was it fear? They kept on walking.

"Easy, men," said Joe.

All at once there was a terrible clang and a sound of rending metal. The head of the mantis appeared in the darkness, looming over the roofs of the smashed cars!

"Get back!" Joe cried.

One of the men let loose a burst from his gun.

The mantis gave an awful bellow and it retreated into the dark.

The mantis appears in the tunnel.

Joe and his men prepare for the final attack.

"After it!" Joe exclaimed. "Get those gas grenades ready!"

The mantis shrieked.

Joe shone his powerful flashlight into the black depths of the tunnel. The light reflected from two huge eyes.

"There it is," Joe shouted. "It's trapped against that pile of wrecked cars! Give it all you've got!"

Outside the tunnel, General Ford, Ned Jackson, and Marge Blaine waited.

They could hear the roars of the trapped monster. They also heard the short burst of gunfire.

"What do you think is happening?" Marge asked fearfully.

An explosion rang out . . . and then another. More sounds of gunfire echoed inside the tunnel. The screams of the deadly mantis became louder and louder.

"I think it's coming this way!" General Ford exclaimed. "Everybody get back!"

Silence settles over the scene of the disaster.

Joe and his men had used all their weapons. They had exploded poison gas grenades and shot the mantis with hundreds of bullets.

"Back outside, men!" Joe shouted. "There's nothing more we can do!"

He and the men dashed back through the tunnel. They could hear the sound of the mantis bellowing behind them. The giant creature was following.

Joe was the last one to reach the entrance. He staggered outside and pulled off the hood of his suit. He stood still, listening.

Everything was quiet.

General Ford, Ned, Marge, and a policeman rushed up.

"Listen!" said Joe. "Do you hear anything?"

The five people were silent. Inside the tunnel, only a few tiny noises could be heard.

"Do you suppose it's dead?" Marge whispered.

"The gas is harmless now," Joe said. "I'm going back inside to look."

"I'll come with you," said Ned.

Marge clutched her camera. "You don't expect me to stay behind, do you?"

There among many smashed cars lay the giant insect. Unmoving.

The deadly mantis appears to be dead.

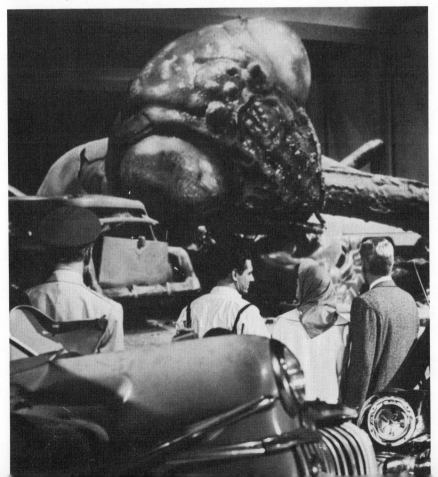

They came close to the creature. Their footsteps echoed in the tunnel. The mantis's head seemed to be as large as a Volkswagen. It had jaws like jointed tentacles. One enormous arm, all studded with spines, lay on the pavement among the wrecked cars.

"How's that for the cover of the museum magazine?" Ned asked jokingly.

Marge looked up at the thing, speechless.

"What are you waiting for?" Joe said with a smile.

Marge hesitates about getting a close-up picture.

The mantis' claw begins to move.

Marge took one small step toward the mantis. She lifted her camera. General Ford came up to speak to Joe. The two of them moved away to confer with the police chief.

Frowning, Marge peered through the viewfinder of her camera. The shot was not quite right. She moved away from Ned, closer to the creature's arm.

"Now I've got it," she said.

Ned cried, "Marge, look out!"

Marge tells Joe it's time to get back to business.

The deadly arm moved up. Its sharp spikes hovered just above Marge's head. She screamed and dropped her camera.

Joe had seen what was happening. "Run, Marge!" he called.

But she seemed paralyzed. Joe raced up to her and scooped her into his arms. He stumbled away as the giant claw chopped down toward them . . . and fell with a harmless crash onto the tunnel pavement!

Marge and Joe were safe. Still in his arms, she turned to him. "You said it was dead!" she said angrily.

"It is dead, Marge," said Ned. "The movement was just a last reflex action. The mantis will never harm anyone again. Thanks to Joe and his men."

"Then I'd better take several pictures of the hero," Marge said. She smiled at Joe. "If he ever gets around to putting me down!"